Dear Parents and Educators,

Welcome to Penguin Young Readers! As parents and educators, you know that each child develops at his or her own pace—in terms of speech, critical thinking, and, of course, reading. Penguin Young Readers recognizes this fact. As a result, each Penguin Young Readers book is assigned a traditional easy-to-read level (1–4) as well as a Guided Reading Level (A–P). Both of these systems will help you choose the right book for your child. Please refer to the back of each book for specific leveling information. Penguin Young Readers features esteemed authors and illustrators, stories about favorite characters, fascinating nonfiction, and more!

Don't Throw It to Mo!

LEVEL **2**

GUIDED READING LEVEL **I**

This book is perfect for a **Progressing Reader** who:
- can figure out unknown words by using picture and context clues;
- can recognize beginning, middle, and ending sounds;
- can make and confirm predictions about what will happen in the text; and
- can distinguish between fiction and nonfiction.

Here are some **activities** you can do during and after reading this book:
- Problem/Solution: The problem in *Don't Throw It to Mo!* is that the other team thinks Mo Jackson is too small to play football. Discuss the solution to the problem, and how Mo Jackson, despite the odds, helps his team win the game.
- Character Traits: In this story, Mo Jackson has many different character traits. Come up with a list of words that describe him.

Remember, sharing the love of reading with a child is the best gift you can give!

—Bonnie Bader, EdM
  Penguin Young Readers program

*Penguin Young Readers are leveled by independent reviewers applying the standards developed by Irene Fountas and Gay Su Pinnell in *Matching Books to Readers: Using Leveled Books in Guided Reading*, Heinemann, 1999.

For my grandson Aaron —DAA

For Janae—SR

ISBN 978-1-338-11837-7

12 11 10 9 8 7 6 5 4 3 2 1   16 17 18 19 20 21

Printed in the U.S.A.   40

First Scholastic printing, September 2016

PENGUIN YOUNG READERS

LEVEL 2
PROGRESSING READER

DON'T THROW IT TO MO!

by David A. Adler
illustrated by Sam Ricks

SCHOLASTIC INC.

Mo Jackson loves football.

When it's time to wake up

his mother calls out,

"It's a long throw."

Mo wakes up.

His mother tosses a football.

Mo jumps out of bed to catch it.

"Now that you're up,"

his mother says,

"get ready for school."

Mo is on the Robins,

a football team.

They practice after school.

Mo is smaller than
the other players.
He's younger.

Mostly, he doesn't play.

He sits on the bench

with Coach Steve.

Sometimes Coach Steve

spreads butter on a football.

"You need to practice holding on

to the ball even if it's slippery."

The Robins are
playing the Jays.

The Jays see Mo and say,

"He's too small to play."

Coach Steve tosses Mo a football.

Mo drops it.

The Jays laugh.

"He's small and he's a butterfingers."

They are right.

The ball he dropped was

Coach Steve's buttered football.

Mo sits on the bench.

He watches the game.

The game is almost over.

The Robins are losing.

"Wash your hands,"

Coach Steve tells Mo.

"Get the butter off.

You're going in."

Coach Steve tells the Robins,
"I'm putting Mo in.
Mo will go deep, but
don't throw to Mo."

The play starts.

Mo runs way out.

A Jay runs with him.

"No one would throw to a small butterfingers," he tells Mo.

He's right.

No one throws to Mo.

It is time for the next play.

"Mo will go deep," Coach Steve

tells the team again.

"But don't throw to Mo."

The play starts.

The same Jay runs with Mo.

Then he stops.

"I'll wait here," he tells Mo.

"No one would throw to

a small butterfingers."

He's right again.

No one throws to Mo.

"This is the last play of the game," Coach Steve tells the team.

"Mo will go deep," he says.

"This time, throw to Mo."

The play starts.

The Jay player runs with Mo.

Then he stops.

But Mo keeps running.

A Robin throws the ball high

over Mo's head.

"He won't get to it,"

the Jays say.

"He's too small."

But Mo does get to the ball.

"He won't catch it,"

the Jays say.

"He's a butterfingers."

But Mo catches it.

He runs with the ball past the
goal line.

The Robins win.

They cheer.

"Coach Steve," Mo says.

"Your plan won the game."

"No, it didn't," the coach says.

"You won the game.

You are the one

who caught the ball."